THE ESSENTIAL GUIDE

Verne is caring, selfless and hard-working, but also a little insecure.

RJ takes life as it comes – but he sometimes takes a little too much!

Hammy has a habit of moving faster than his brain.

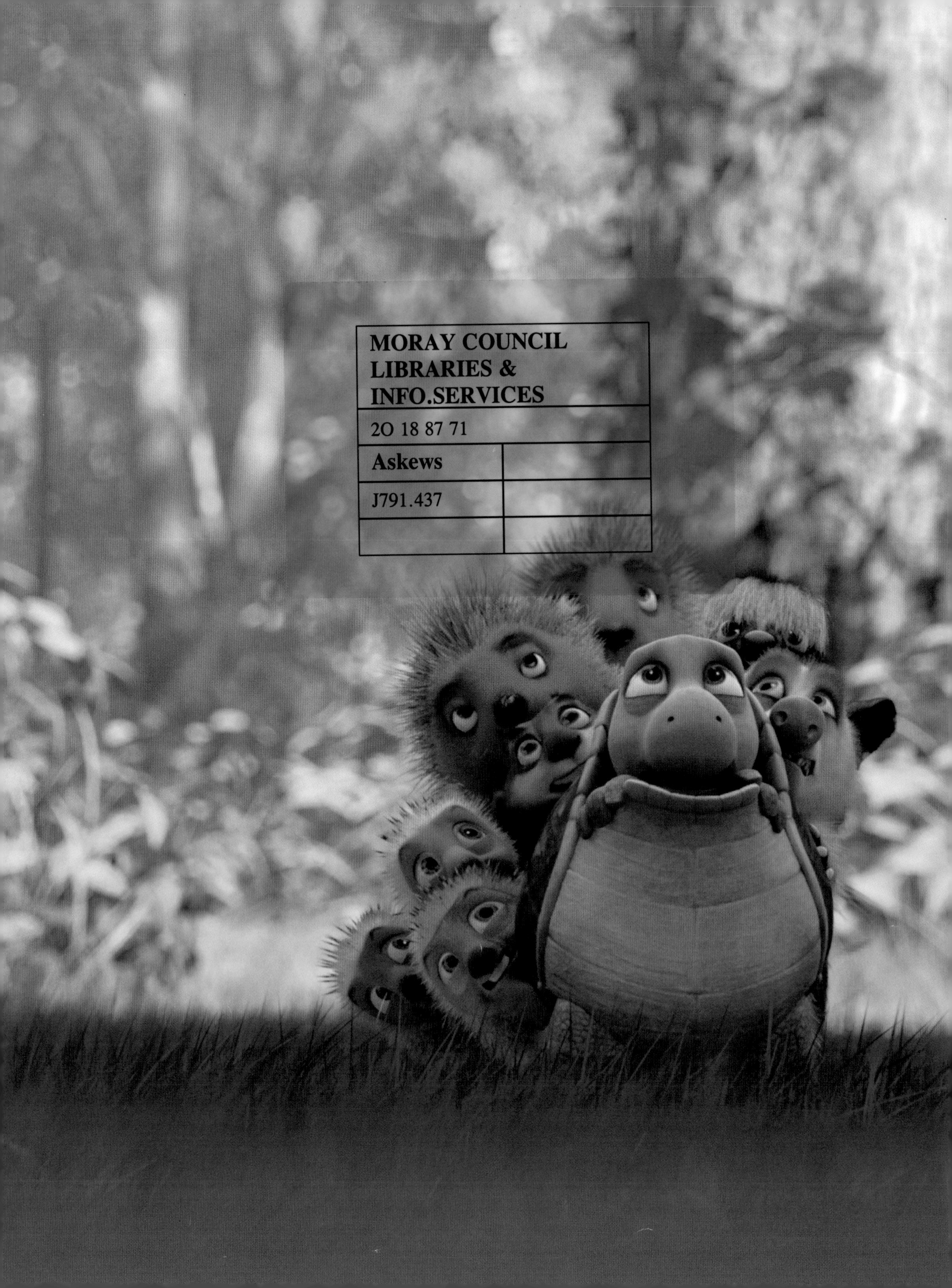

DREAMWORKS
OVER THE HEDGE™

THE ESSENTIAL GUIDE

CONTENTS

The Stash	6	Gladys' Rules of Suburbia	28
RJ	8	Foraging for Food	30
Verne	10	The Heists	32
Hammy	12	Nugent	34
Heather & Ozzie	14	Up, Up & Away	36
Stella	16	Dwayne	38
Porcupine Family	18	RJ's Big Plan	40
The Hedge	20	Stella Makes Her Move	42
El Rancho Camelot Estates	22	Forest Family	44
This Way to the Food	24	Happy Together	46
Gladys	26		

THE STASH

The blue cooler keeps Vincent's drinks nice and chilled.

R J the raccoon is used to living on scraps or stealing from vending machines. But after a hard winter, scraps are scarce and the vending machines aren't being as helpful as usual. So he takes a big risk: he steals Vincent the bear's food stash!

A hungry raccoon has to be brave or desperate to enter a sleeping bear's cave. What RJ finds there makes his eyes pop!

Vincent's stash has taken him all year to collect.

Junk mountain

Potato crisps, cereals, cookies and a dozen types of drink – Vincent's mountain of junk food is enough to set RJ's heart racing, his stomach rumbling and his brain working double-time!

Vincent's most prized possession is his red wagon.

Raccoons are known for their dexterity and agility, but by piling all of the food into the red wagon, RJ sets some kind of world record!

BUSTED!

RJ likes to think big – unfortunately for him that usually means getting into big trouble! Unable to resist sampling a fresh tube of crisps, RJ wakes the sleeping Vincent and lands himself in a bear-sized mess of trouble!

Even though he's already got a wagon full of food, RJ can't resist trying to take one more snack – only to wake the sleeping bear.

The only way RJ can stay off Vincent's menu is to replace all the food, the wagon and the cooler, too!

I'M JUST A DESPERATE GUY TRYING TO FEED HIS FAMILY... A FAMILY OF ONE!

The pile of junk food contains five kinds of cookies.

RJ

A charming, small-time scavenger, RJ the raccoon is used to living on his wits. Unfortunately, his smart mouth and love of a scam land him in trouble more often than not.

So much to do

RJ is given a week to replace the stash of food he stole from Vincent the bear. Luckily, this raccoon has always been a people person – that is, he's always been good at stealing food from people!

Racoon Fact

Raccoons are omnivores, which means they will eat anything – and that includes anything left in a rubbish bin.

Has RJ bitten off more than he can chew by crossing Vincent? Well, if there's one thing this Raccoon's good at, it's chewing.

Feet used to scamper from trouble.

UNDER CONTROL

- RJ never goes anywhere without his golf bag. It contains all the tools a resourceful raccoon needs to get by in the wild; a toy fishing reel, a grabber arm... and a golf club.

- RJ's nimble forepaws enable him to open packets and cans, just like human beings. But the most nimble part of his body is his brain – he can think his way out of trouble in a flash.

- Unfortunately, he's also really good at thinking himself into trouble in the first place!

Golf bag doubles as a handy food store.

Ringed tail – used for balance when climbing.

YOU JUST REST EASY, 'CAUSE I'M ON IT.

Wagon hunt

RJ even has to replace Vincent's bright red wagon. Luckily, this raccoon's a strong believer in "Finders Keepers"... just so long as the owner's not looking.

VERNE

Verne is a responsible turtle who takes his job as head of the family very seriously. He wants to make sure there's enough food to last through the next winter – even though the last winter has only just finished!

Foraging time

When the animals come out of hibernation and begin foraging for food, Verne says the same thing every single year: "Eat one, save two".

The American box turtle has four fingers and toes on each hand and foot.

Protective shell

I'M A REPTILE ACTUALLY. IT'S A COMMON MISTAKE.

Arms and legs can be pulled right inside his shell.

Verne is a steady, "one-step-at-a-time" kind of turtle. It may not be fast or flashy, but it gets him where he wants to go.

Verne is the first to venture through the hedge. What he sees on the other side changes the lives of all the woodland animals.

Turtle Fact

The shell of a box turtle is strong enough to support a weight more than 200 times greater than itself!

Softer undershell or plastron

When Verne tries to return the stolen food, he breaks the World Turtle Speed Record.

TINGLING TAIL

- Verne has his own built-in alarm system. Whenever there's danger lurking or trouble brewing, his tail starts to tingle.

- Like other turtles, Verne can duck inside his shell for protection.

- He might be cautious, but Verne's no scaredy-shell or timid turtle. He's willing to face up to anything to help his friends... even a cunning raccoon!

HAMMY

Hammy the squirrel is as over-stimulated as a child on too much sugar… and that's before he's even tasted the stuff! None of the other forest animals has feet as fast, or an attention span as short!

More please!

Hammy has a habit of saying exactly what's on his mind the moment it arrives there. This means he'll often blurt something out without thinking, but he never means any harm.

Squirrel Fact

A squirrel's eyes are high on each side of its head. This gives it a wide field of vision, without having to turn around.

Hammy is curious and hungry for new experiences. He's also happy to leap into any situation without thinking – which makes him the perfect sidekick for the reckless RJ!

Long toes for climbing

HAMMY TIME

- According to naturalists, a squirrel's brain is the size of a walnut. In Hammy's case, this is probably an exaggeration!

- Like all squirrels, Hammy is fast and agile, with a real knack for getting into and out of tight spaces.

- A simple guy, all Hammy craves is love and attention... and cookies... and nachos... and doughnuts... and cola... and sugar... lots and lots of sugar!

A squirrel's tail is also used when swimming.

Tails provide balance while climbing and jumping.

I AM A CRAZY RABBIT-SQUIRREL!

Face to face

Hammy loves people food so much that he's ready to take on anyone to defend his cookies – even his own reflection!

13

HEATHER & OZZIE

Like all teenagers, Heather is embarrassed by her dad, Ozzie, and his act. However, Ozzie is proud of his family's long tradition of playing dead to fool predators.

Opossums have acute hearing.

Ozzie

Ozzie has spent years honing his act – but his daughter wants nothing to do with it. He knows that one day Heather's life may depend upon playing dead... and he's right!

DROP DEAD!

- Ozzie is anxious that Heather should practise playing dead, but Heather would rather give a predator her sulky stare!

- When Heather comes face-to-face with Gladys, she does what comes naturally – she plays dead! Ozzie is so proud of his little girl.

ISN'T PLAYING DEAD A LITTLE – WEAK?

Opossum Fact

Opossums don't just play dead. When attacked, they will also bare their 52 sharp teeth, growl and drool (ick!).

Heather's special sulky stare.

The in-betweener

Heather's too old to fool around with Quillo, Spike and Bucky, the three porcupine kids, and she figures the grown-ups are much too old to hang with.

Opossum fur can be white, black or grey.

Opossum's are North America's only native marsupial species.

Good show!

Even though she doesn't want to get in on the family act, Heather is impressed when her father performs an over-the-top performance as roadkill.

STELLA

Stella is a straight-talking skunk with an attitude more powerful than her foul-smelling spray. But when she's given a chance to save her friends, she really struts her stuff.

If this end is pointing your way – run!

Skunk fur can be brown as well as black.

When she thinks the hedge has eaten Verne, Stella gets ready to let rip.

Hunger!

Stella believes in standing by her friends and usually trusts Verne's tingling tail – but even she can't resist the junk food RJ introduces to them.

MASTER BLASTER

- Stella always says exactly what she thinks and expects everyone else to do the same. She has no time for fools, but can be hardest of all on herself.

- Stella's straight-talking is sometimes just a cover for her real feelings. Being a skunk can be tough when your stink gets in the way of true love.

- Could Stella have found romance with Tiger – a cat that can't smell?

Stella envies the sweet perfume of flowers.

Stella's makeover

To get to the food in Gladys' kitchen, the animals have to get past Gladys' fierce cat, Tiger. Luckily, RJ has a plan that will turn Stella from skunk to glamour puss in order to woo the fearsome feline!

THERE'S MORE WHERE THAT CAME FROM, PUFFBALL!

With the help of a handy compact disc, RJ persuades Stella that she really needs a makeover.

Skunk Fact

Skunks aim their spray at an attacker's face. It causes extreme irritation, and even temporary blindness!

PORCUPINE FAMILY

Lou and Penny are a rock-solid Midwestern couple who are devoted to their kids, Spike, Quillo and Bucky, and their kids are devoted to having fun!

Mum and Dad

Penny and Lou love the routines of family life and looking after their three noisy kids. Lou might be prickly but he's very easy-going!

Whenever full-time mum, Penny, needs a break, Lou is happy to look after the kids.

Porcupine quills are only used in self-defence.

JEEPERS IS THE WORD, HON.

PLAY TIME

- The first thing Spike, Quillo and Bucky want to do when they wake up is play. It's the last thing they do before going to sleep, too!

- The kids quickly become computer game experts, working together to operate all of the console's buttons.

Their favourite game? Auto Homicide 3!

Porcupine Fact

Porcupines have over 30,000 quills! Each quill is 7.5 cm (3 in) long and black in colour, with a yellowish tip.

Young porcupines' quills harden within an hour after birth.

THE HEDGE

Where does it come from? What does it want? Does it have a name? All these questions run through the minds of Verne and the animals. But there's one thing they all know for sure: it wasn't there when they went to sleep, last winter!

None of them has ever seen a bush so long that even super-fast Hammy can't find the end.

Ozzie plays dead as soon as he hears strange and frightening voices from the other side of the hedge.

Introducing...

... RJ – who offers to explain the mysteries of the hedge and what lies beyond to the bewildered group of forest animals.

Hedge Fact

Hedges have been used to mark boundaries since the time of the Roman Empire, over 2,000 years ago!

What's on the other side?

There could be anything on the other side of the hedge. The animals hear angry voices, weird clangs and loud roars. Even when Hammy calls the hedge "Steve", it still seems strange and scary.

Hedges can be made from shrubs or small trees.

OH, GREAT AND POWERFUL STEVE!

Ozzie bows down in front of Steve the hedge to ask what it wants.

ONE SMALL STEP

While the other animals stare in awe and wonder, Verne realises that there is only one way to solve the mystery of Steve the hedge and that's to find out what's on the other side. It's a big step for a little turtle... and a giant leap into the unknown!

El Rancho Camelot Estates

No trees! No berry bushes! And definitely no wildlife! Just acres of gardens, thousands of square metres of houses and tarmac-covered road as far as the eye can see. Welcome to paradise!

From RJ's map, the animals can see they are surrounded by a suburban nightmare.

Lighting makes the houses look inviting at night – even more so when the animals realise that they're full of food.

Welcome to suburbia!

El Rancho Camelot is the latest in a long line of developed suburbs. It is the perfect place for families who want to escape from the city to a place in the country... just so long as "the country" still has modern roads, electricity and central heating.

The only frogs allowed in El Rancho Camelot are the kind that water the lawns.

All exteriors must be decorated with the same shade of paint.

SUVs are available in a range of colours, as long as they blend tastefully with the surroundings.

Rancho Fact

By the time the builders have finished painting the last house to be built, it's time to re-paint the first house!

22

MANICURED, MAN-MADE PARADISE!

All the roofs slope at the same precise angle.

HOME SWEET HOME

Every house in El Rancho Camelot is a state-of-the-art family dwelling: temperature-controlled, air-conditioned, triple-glazed and sound-proofed. Local by-laws restrict lawn height, house decorations and holding noisy parties.

Metal, termite-proof letterbox post.

Every home is fitted with the latest coffee maker.

The Camelot Observer

THIS WAY TO THE FOOD

A life spent scavenging in back yards has given RJ a personal view of humans and their food. He has come to one simple conclusion: animals eat to live, humans live to eat.

YOU THINK THEY HAVE ENOUGH?... THEY HAVE TOO MUCH!

What a waste!

RJ has seen how much food humans eat... and how much they throw away. It seems only natural that he should be able to take advantage of humans' wastefulness.

The animals stare in disbelief as a truck opens to reveal a whole mountain of food that Gladys is having delivered for a party she's holding.

Gladys believes rubbish should stay inside the bins – something RJ is about to change!

RJ – tour guide of the trash – explains that the food in these silver bins is put there for the animals' benefit.

According to RJ, the front door is used for one thing: letting more food into the house.

Is it a taco? Is it a truck? And why would you want to drive a taco when you could eat one instead? According to RJ, it just shows how crazy human beings are about food.

As well as using machines to drive from place to place (RJ figures this is because they are losing the use of their legs), humans also spend hours riding machines that don't go anywhere – just so they can eat more food!

CHOW TIME!

RJ's study of the human beings that live in El Rancho Camelot reveals that they are surrounded by so much food that they have almost stopped noticing it – unless their pizza delivery is late or there are no more cookies in the cupboard, that is!

Pizza – round food in a square box.

PAUL'S PIZZERIA
PAUL'S PIZZE

Submarine sandwich – dive, dive... diet!

GLADYS

Every community needs a leader and Gladys has decided that she is it. To her, El Rancho Camelot is perfect and she'll do anything to keep it that way.

Critter carnage

Gladys cannot stand chaos and disorder, and she is driven mad by the forest animals when they descend on El Rancho Camelot. For her there is only one option, and that's to call in Dwayne!

Gladys believes in making her point forcefully.

Gladys makes it clear to Dwayne that she wants to see results – and that means dead animals!

26

I LOVE SUV

Gladys' SUV (Sports Utility Vehicle) is her pride and joy. It guzzles petrol by the litre, takes up a huge amount of space and belches harmful fumes into the air. In other words, it's greedy, loud and full of hot air – just like its owner!

Blacked out windows for extra style

Black is Gladys' favourite colour.

Gladys uses super-strong hairspray to keep every hair in the right place.

Tiger

There is one animal that Gladys adores – her over-fed Persian cat, Tiger, whose full name is Prince Tigeriess Mahmood Shabaz. Tiger is able to come and go as he pleases, thanks to a high-tech cat flap and electronic key on his collar.

The high-tech key to the most high-tech cat flap in El Rancho Camelot.

Gladys Fact

Gladys can take a phone call, write a shopping list and create a new rule for the Homeowners Association – all while driving her SUV!

27

GLADYS' RULES OF SUBURBIA

What is the secret of a happy peaceful community? Happy families? Friendly neighbours? Clean air and open spaces where children can play? Gladys Sharp knows: rules, rules... and more rules!

Gladys' house – headquarters of the El Rancho Camelot Homeowners' Association.

Rules

At the last count, the El Rancho Camelot Homeowners' Charter contained 765 rules. That's a lot, but Gladys knows every one by heart – because she wrote most of them!

Lifelike animal-shaped bushes set Dwayne's trigger finger twitching.

THIS IS GLADYS SHARP. YOUR PRESIDENT.

Suburban Fact
The word "suburb" comes from the Latin word "suburbium", which means "near to a city".

Gladys' flamingo lawn ornaments are so lifelike that Dwayne "traps" one by mistake.

Garden ornament or a booby trap? By the time an animal discovers the truth, it's too late!

BY THE BOOK

According to Gladys there are three things that will spoil El Rancho Camelot for everyone: unauthorised gatherings, overgrown lawns... and people (and animals) who break the rules! Her most recent additions to the Homeowners' Charter are:

DO remove all floating leaves from your pool before 8 am.

DON'T allow your pool water temperature to vary from 30.4°C.

DO make sure that your grass is exactly 5 centimetres tall – 6 centimetres is not acceptable.

DO make sure that rubbish bins are placed 1 metre from the kerb.

DON'T put out your rubbish until 7 am.

DO check with the President before holding a barbecue, summer party, bonfire party, Christmas party, birthday party... or any other kind of party.

DON'T forget: the President's decision is final!

FORAGING FOR FOOD

While humans feast, animals forage, hunt and scavenge. Since the humans have more food than they need, RJ doesn't see anything wrong in causing chaos throughout El Rancho Camelot in his quest for something to eat!

To RJ, cookies are more valuable than gold.

The raccoon with a plan.

Cookie box: easy for a nimble-fingered raccoon to open.

Cookie catcher

RJ's first target is a wagon-load of Trail Guide Gals cookies. Hammy is happy to help out – he'll do anything to get a taste of yummy cookie!

WAS I RIGHT OR WAS I RIGHT?

Humans like Gladys think it's rubbish, but the forest animals have never seen so much food. It doesn't take much for RJ to persuade them to steal more human food – all except for Verne who wants to forage the old-fashioned way.

Hammy in cookie heaven.

LIVING OFF THE LAND

• In the forest, the animals have to chew bark and eat berries and leaves. Verne is convinced that this is the right way.

• He is certain it's better to live off the land rather than scavenge among the humans' garbage. But even he has to admit those cookies are pretty tasty!

Sharp-tasting berries

Food Fact

There are six main food groups: proteins, carbohydrates, fats, fibre, minerals and vitamins. Cookies are not a food group!

THE HEISTS

The humans have all the junk food RJ needs – all he has to do is find a way to get his paws on it! He and the other animals stage some daring heists.

Heist one

Trail Guide Gals cookies are at the top of RJ's must-have list. As the girls go door-to-door delivering cookies, RJ and Hammy spring into action.

Trail Guide Handbook – essential for every girl in the field.

Trail Guide Gals wagon – essential for carrying cookies.

Hammy's a natural-born actor – even if he's not sure whether he's playing a crazy rabid squirrel or a crazy rabbit-squirrel.

Verne comes to Hammy's rescue – but manages to lose his shell in the process. A naked turtle's a pretty weird sight – just ask Shelby the Trail Guide Gal!

Heist two

Stealing a cooler from the roof of a moving SUV seems an impossible challenge, but not when you've got RJ's scheming scavenger's brain and Ozzie's acting talents!

The human cooler is identical to Vincent's.

Ozzie gives the performance of a lifetime: a three-act death scene complete with speeches and bright lights.

While Ozzie's "dying", RJ and the others steal the cooler. All eyes are on Ozzie's performance as RJ's plan comes together.

The cooler makes a great hiding place.

NUGENT

Nugent the rottweiler is a loyal, friendly and good-natured dog... he's just not too bright! He loves two things most in the world: sleeping and playing – unfortunately he only knows how to play rough!

RJ tries to talk Verne out of returning all of the stolen food. Neither of them realises that big, rottweiler-shaped trouble's just around the corner.

Rottweilers have a thick coat of coarse red-brown fur.

The moment Nugent hears one of his squeak-toys, all he wants to do is play!

Play time

Nugent thinks Verne wants to play.
Nugent thinks everybody wants to
play – but Verne only wants to be like
Ozzie and Heather... and play dead!

*Rottweilers are very loyal
and usually form a strong
bond with one person.*

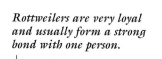

PLAY! PLAY! PLAY! PLAY! PLAY!

Verne's lesson

Verne takes a valuable lesson away
from his meeting with Nugent:
rottweilers run faster than turtles...
especially turtles wearing squeak-
toys for running shoes!

*A turtle
playing
possum.*

*Nugent needs a
stronger chain to keep
him in his garden.*

Rottweiler Fact

*Rottweilers
originated in Italy.
Their ancestors
accompanied
Roman armies
2,000 years ago!*

Up, Up & Away

Verne decides to return the food that the animals have taken. He realises that their light-fingered antics have attracted the wrong sort of attention in the form of Gladys and Dwayne La Fontaine.

The only way is up!

A red wagon piled with a blue cooler and a mountain of snacks is not the most aerodynamic vehicle. But add a lawn mower, sun lounger and the gas canister from a neighbour's barbecue, and Verne and RJ are ready for lift-off... whether they like it or not!

This stash of food is about to become the in-flight menu.

The trouble starts when RJ tries to stop Verne from returning the food. The two start squabbling and this noise wakes up Nugent who thinks it's play time.

MY ENTIRE SHELL IS TINGLING!

Barbecue gas canister engine.

The slide in a neighbour's garden makes a perfect launch-ramp for the air-bound wagon and its test pilots: Verne and RJ!

Sun lounger acts as wings.

RJ and Verne boldly go where no raccoon or turtle have ever gone before. And all without seat belts, crash helmets... or any idea of how they're going to get down!

Animal armageddon

Any landing you can walk away from is a good landing. RJ, Verne, the other animals and the inhabitants of El Rancho Camelot might not be so sure after this landing though!

DWAYNE

Dwayne's weak eyes are due to years spent squinting at animal tracks.

Dwayne La Fontaine has dedicated his life to the extermination of vermin, large and small. RJ, Verne and the others are next on his list!

Dwayne assures Gladys that he has the tools and know-how to rid El Rancho Camelot of its "animal problem".

Trap happy

Dwayne believes in exterminating vermin by any means necessary and will use every tool and trick in the book. His high-tech traps soon turn Gladys' back yard into a war zone!

Even Ozzie's greatest performance isn't good enough to fool Dwayne.

DWAYNE'S BATTLE BUS

High-tech bug-zapper

Dwayne's logo

- Dwayne travels everywhere in his customised pest control truck – it has been weeks since he last slept in his apartment. The truck is packed with every kind of animal trap and extermination device – including the awesome Depelter Turbo (illegal in 48 states in the USA).

- The truck is fitted with state-of-the-art tracking technology, from radar and infrared to DNA analysers and animal fur colour charts.

Bull bars

ANIMAL PROBLEM? THE SOLUTION IS STANDING BEFORE YOU!

Dwayne Fact

Dwayne's nose is so sensitive that he is able to distinguish the scents of 500 different species of vermin.

Dwayne creeps through El Rancho Camelot after dark, net gun at the ready, sniffing out vermin to trap, transfer and (Dwayne's favorite "T") terminate.

RJ'S BIG PLAN

RJ's plan is simple. Phase one – kill the lights, get past the garden's traps and alarms, distract Tiger the cat, run through the locked cat flap and into Gladys' kitchen...

RJ outlines his plan.

Phase two

... collect all the food, then make it out through the cat flap, get past Tiger (again), get past the traps and alarms (again and again) and get safely back over the hedge. What could be easier?

These cookie boxes are empty but Gladys' kitchen is full.

The key

Tiger's collar electronically unlocks the spoilt kitty's cat flap. It's the only way into the kitchen. Stella doesn't realise it, but she's going to play a vital role in making RJ's plan happen.

Verne wonders how he got into this.

Nobody wants to be the boot in RJ's plan.

Bucky, Spike and Quillo all want to be the car.

STELLA MAKES HER MOVE

Tiger jealously guards his comfortable life with Gladys. He's not a kitty to mess with!

There's only one way into Gladys' kitchen: through Tiger's electronic-locking cat flap. And the only way to open that is with an electronic key that's hung around Tiger's neck!

Tiger's secret

Tiger is a cat with a secret: he suffers from terrible allergies that have robbed him of his sense of smell. Little does he suspect that those same allergies make him the man of Stella's dreams!

Glamour puss

Tiger makes a big mistake when he calls Stella a common stray. There is nothing common about this skunk-turned-pussycat! Tiger falls for her shoot-from-the-lip attitude.

The electronic key to the high-tech cat flap hangs from Tiger's collar.

Stella slips Tiger's collar off with ease.

Verne and the others see a whole new side to Stella as she puts the moves on Tiger.

All too easy

Verne's still not sure RJ's plan is going to work... right up to the moment Tiger's collar lands in his hand. The animals hustle inside while Stella keeps the pussycat occupied.

I GOT MAKE-UP ON MY BUTT, DUDE!

Stella's skunk stripes are hidden by make up.

FOREST FAMILY

The animals wake to find their forest has been changed by the arrival of the humans. In this new world, they have to learn new ways to get along... with the humans and each other.

RJ came looking for a way to save his life from Vincent. The last thing he expected to find was a family.

A new way?

Verne believes that the family that forages together stays together. RJ shows him that the family that raids the garbage and takes cookies is guaranteed to have the adventure of a lifetime!

Stella discovers that there really is someone for everyone – all she has to do is be herself.

Verne discovers that when his tail tingles it can sometimes mean adventure is right around the corner.

44

The next generation

Lou and Penny always thought their kids would grow up in a world just like the one they knew. But it's the computer game-playing youngsters that steer the whole forest family towards a happy – if bumpy – ending.

Hammy didn't think he could be any more hyperactive – then he unleashes his sugar-fuelled inner action hero to save the day.

From sulky teen to dying queen – Heather discovers that she has inherited her dad's acting talent... and it's a real life-saver!

Ozzie gives the performance of his life – but it's Heather's first ever performance that makes him the proudest possum in the pack!

HAPPY TOGETHER

As RJ meets Vincent to repay his debt of food, the fast-talking raccoon discovers that he cares a whole lot more about his new forest family than he thought possible.

THIS WHOLE FAMILY THING IS VERY CONFUSING.

Vincent hits suburbia

Vincent the angry – and hungry – bear hits suburbia with a bang in pursuit of RJ and his food. Meanwhile, RJ struggles to free Verne and the others from Dwayne's cages as the porcupine kids steer his runaway truck.

RJ has a new family – but that won't stop him from coming up with some new schemes.

Verne welcomes RJ into the forest family.

Hammy time!

The already-hyperactive Hammy gets a jolt to a whole new level when he gets his first taste of cola. The world around him slows to a crawl – only he has the speed to save everyone from Vincent, Gladys, Dwayne and the Depelter Turbo!

Hammy's already looking forward to the next cookie heist.

Raccoons are resourceful, but RJ is the first raccoon to use a fishing rod!

NATURE

- Raccoons are good at tipping over rubbish bins to get at the discarded food inside.
- Squirrels are agile and will use any means to steal food from bird tables or feeders.
- Opossums like to nest in the warm attics under roofs. The noise they make can keep the homeowners awake at night!

Happily ever after

Vincent, Dwayne and Gladys suffer the fate of the Depelter Turbo. As the authorities take Gladys and Vincent away, Dwayne tries to sneak off, but only gets as far as the garden of playful Nugent! The forest family watch all the action in safety, knowing that their numbers have swelled by one with the welcome addition of RJ.

Stella's ready to get re-acquainted with Tiger!

47

LONDON, NEW YORK, MUNICH,
MELBOURNE and DELHI

Created by Tall Tree Ltd
For DK
Publishing Manager Simon Beecroft
Category Publisher Alex Allan
Brand Manager Rob Perry
Editor Amy Junor
DTP Designer Lauren Egan
Production Rochelle Talary

First published in the UK in 2006 by
Dorling Kindersley Limited
80 Strand, London WC2R 0RL
A Penguin Company

06 07 08 10 9 8 7 6 5 4 3 2 1

Over The Hedge TM and © 2006 DreamWorks Animation L.L.C.
Page Design Copyright © 2006 Dorling Kindersley

A CIP catalogue record for this book is available from the British Library.

ISBN 1-4053-1422-2

High-resolution workflow proofed by Media Development and Printing Ltd, UK
Printed and bound in Italy by L.E.G.O.

Dorling Kindersley would like to thank:
Corinne Combs, Kristy Cox and Rhion Magee

Discover more at
www.dk.com